> *There are more things in earth, Horatio,*
>
> *Than are dreamt of in your philosophy.*

Hamlet to Horatio
Hamlet, William Shakespeare

> *I have never experienced anything like it in my life before.*

Police Officer

> *I felt an evil presence watching me.*

Police Officer

> *None of us could believe our eyes when the bottle flew across the briefing room . . .*

Police Sergeant

MANY THANKS TO THE FOLLOWING FOR THEIR CONTRIBUTIONS:

Dr Martin Baines QPM., Director of Bradford Police Museum
Natalie Baines, Curator of Bradford Police Museum
Steve Longbottom and Mark Plovie, City Centre Beat
West Yorkshire Police
Sarah Howsen, Bradford Council
The staff of Bradford Council

First Publication August 2015
Second Publication March 2016

Published by **Spectral ▼ Books**

www.spectralbooks.com

All rights reserved ©Les Vasey. Except as provided by the Copyright Act, no part of this publication may be reproduced, stored in a retrieval system or transmitted in any form or by any means without the prior written permission of the publisher.

The views expressed do not represent those of the Society for Psychical Research.

CONTENTS

PREFACE	5
INTRODUCTION	6
THE CELLS	8
THE BRADFORD COURT ROOM	10
CHANGES	11
A SQUATTER?	12
THE POLICE MUSEUM	14
AN INVESTIGATION	16
NOTES: POLICE DEPARTMENT	17
NOTES: CITY HALL AND COURTS	21
NOTES: MUSEUM AND CELLS	27
FINDINGS	31
ABOUT THE AUTHOR	32
APPENDIX 1: DEATHS IN CUSTODY	33

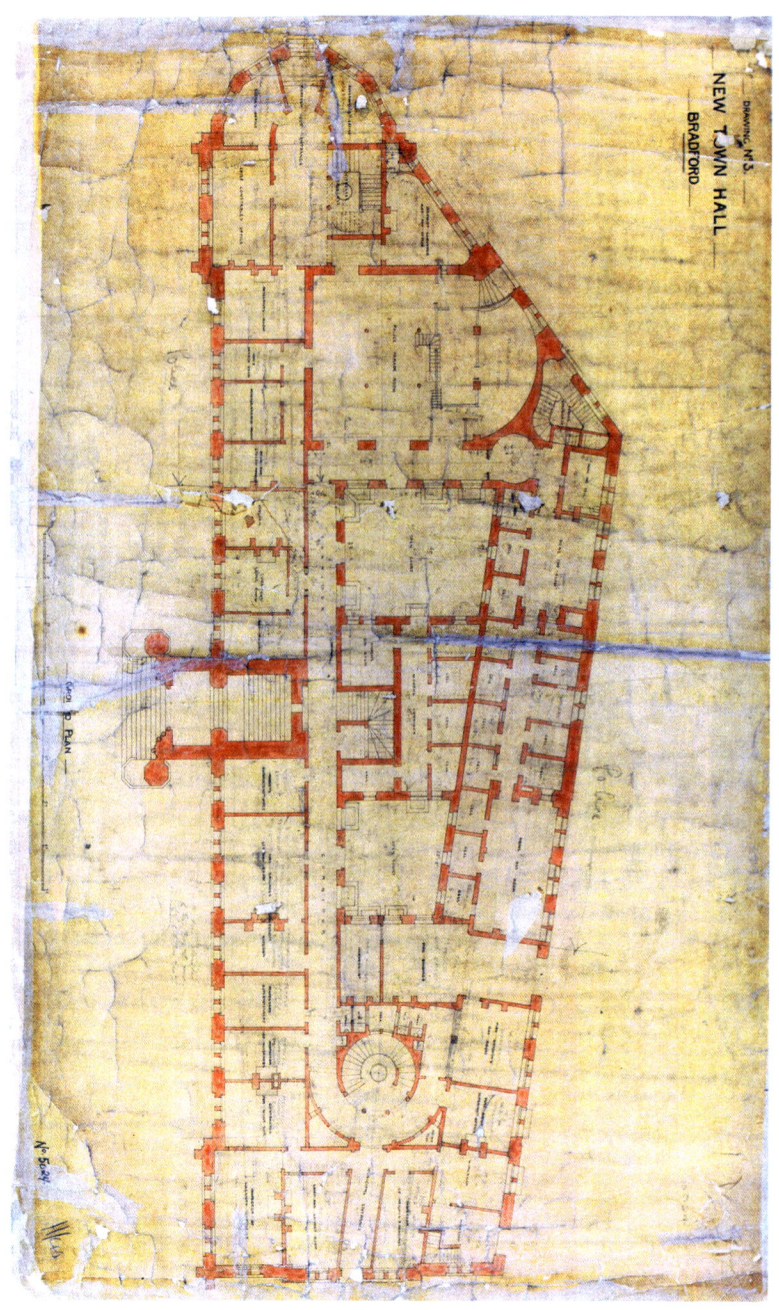

Old plan of Town Hall circa 1873

PREFACE

I never used to believe in ghosts. I was a bit of a sceptic, to be honest. Sometimes I would watch supernatural-themed TV shows, like 'Most Haunted', but I wasn't convinced by what I saw. Although intriguing, it all seemed a bit too far-fetched for me. So when I heard about the strange events I am about to relate I thought there would be some rational explanations. After all what are poltergeists?

The whole subject of poltergeist activity has been investigated over many years. One of the most authoritative bodies is The Society for Psychical Research. Founded in 1882, it has published an impressive body of evidence in relation to the occurrence of paranormal activity.

There have been a number of high profile investigations of these phenomena in various locations across the world. One of the most extraordinary recent cases was the Enfield Poltergeist, the subject of a film and TV series by the same name.

Having spent decades as a police officer interviewing witnesses I was well aware of how fickle the human mind is when recounting and interpreting experiences. I therefore needed some convincing that there was a ghost in Bradford City Hall.

The challenge to any investigation is to find credible forensic corroboration of an allegation. Often the investigator is only left with the testimony of a single witness. This is often the case in reports of paranormal activity. Therefore the credibility of the witness is crucial. In my investigation into these events I have been very impressed by the quality of the witnesses I spoke to and their apparent sincerity.

In the absence of any obvious motives and in view of their professional status, it was difficult not to believe the accounts of the witnesses. Although they made no request for me to do so, I have kept the names of the witnesses confidential.

I thank all those who participated in this enquiry for their courage and openness in relating their experiences to me. Without their contribution I could not have written this book.

INTRODUCTION

*B*radford's magnificent City Hall holds some dark secrets...
It is an old building that still retains much of its Victorian history, particularly relating to the former police cells and the court. There are areas where 'ghostly apparitions' have been reported and where 'poltergeist activity' is still taking place.

Built in 1873, it was originally designed to provide facilities for the Bradford Borough Police and the Law Courts. For the next hundred years, the new Borough Police Headquarters would have a purpose built cell block, a parade room, offices, and facilities for the police surgeon. The design of the charge office and cells enabled prisoners to be processed from the reception point to detention, trial and sentencing in the same building.

Over the years thousands of prisoners, including men, women and children, would have been locked up in Bradford's dark and eerie cells.
Most of them went on to face court proceedings and sentencing without ever leaving the building.

Often these desolate individuals were there due to their circumstances. The poverty and hunger that existed in Bradford in Victorian times must have often driven people to crime.

Many would have been locked up for petty offences such as begging, prostitution or stealing food. Penalties were however harsh and included lengthy jail sentences. Some prisoners detained for more serious crimes such as murder, would have faced the prospect of the gallows if subsequently convicted.

Eleven Bradford prisoners would ultimately face the hangman for their crimes.

It is said that the ghost of one such prisoner, who died on the scaffold, returns to the place of his incarceration to bemoan his fate. Like the ghost of Jacob Marley he drags with him the chains of his former life.

BRADFORD PRISONERS EXECUTED: 1873 TO 1954

John Henry Johnson	3rd April 1877
James Harrison	26th August 1890
Walter Robinson	17th August 1897
John William Ellwood	3rd December 1908
John Roper Coulson	9th August 1910
William Horsley Wardell	18th June 1924
John Henry Roberts	28th April 1932
Lewis Hamilton	6th April 1934
Arthur Thompson	31st January 1945
William Batty	8th January 1946
Edward Lindsey Reid	1st September 1954

THE CELLS

I brought my first prisoner to the charge office desk as a young constable in 1968. Even then, the charge office and cells were a daunting place to enter. I thought how archaic and foreboding they looked.

The Victorian charge office and cell area still remain intact. They are now part of the Victorian police museum in City Hall. The visitor can still walk along the same passageway that took the prisoners from the charge desk to the cell block and visit the same gloomy, insanitary, cells where prisoners once languished.

Along the corridor gaunt faces of former inmates stare back from the Victorian rogues' gallery of photographs pinned to the wall.

Men, women and adolescents with hopeless expressions on their faces.

A 1901 leaflet, advertising performances of Houdini the escapologist adorns a nearby wall, near the cell where from where he allegedly escaped. A life size poster of a former Victorian hangman and constable, James Berry, holding a shackled youngster is prominently displayed in the cell passage.

Hazy light from the small barred windows barely penetrates the gloom of the cells. The heavy steel door

Rogues gallery

and the four stone walls would confine the prisoner until his trial.

There they would have languished, fearfully contemplating their fate; traumatised by the smells, the clanging of doors, the rattling of chains and heavy keys.

Sometimes, prisoners, already in poor physical and mental health, expired whilst in custody. Others committed suicide. (See Appendix 1)

The visitor can still feel the same uncompromising, harsh environment of all those years ago. The noises and smells have gone, but the oppressive atmosphere remains. Sometimes cold chills and sinister shadows continue to unsettle visitors and guides alike as they tour the cell area.

THE BRADFORD COURT ROOM

On court days prisoners were taken from their separate cells to the large day cell. There, they were temporarily held; their names and charges called out as they were named and shamed. They would then be led, sometimes in chains, along a passageway to the ominous, steep metal staircase which would lead to the dock, to face their fate in number one court.

The Bradford number one court served as both a Magistrates Court, that sat most days and a court of Quarter Sessions, that sat periodically and tried more serious indictable offences.

In the brass-railed dock of the majestic court room, prisoners were arraigned before the presiding judge or magistrate. With its high gothic windows, fine wood panelling and ornate mouldings, the contrast with the bleak cells would have been awe inspiring.

It is said that the walls still retain and occasionally replay the historic trials that took place there.

From time to time it has been reported that ghostly entities from the past return to re-enact the trials of yester-years.

Staircase to court

CHANGES

In 1974, following police boundary changes, the Bradford City Police was amalgamated with the West Yorkshire force. Thus ended over 100 years of police history as the members of the force ended their ties with their Victorian past and left their old home in City Hall.

Along with the magistrates they were relocated to brand new, modern accommodation at the Tyrls. Even the cell areas were brighter with much improved facilities. The empty and forsaken dusty corridors and offices where the police had once performed their duties were abandoned.

They would eventually be sub-divided and converted into modern, brighter office accommodation for the expanding number of council departments and staff. Significantly the changes had also encroached onto the old cell area.

It seems however that not everyone was happy to leave. Someone or something from those old police days had decided to stay behind.

Leaving City Hall

A SQUATTER?

Over the following years, reports of 'ghostly' apparitions and psychic activity were reported in various locations, including the courts, the cells, and the toilets and in the former police areas. The entity believed responsible for the strange and disturbing activities was and is still known as 'Chains Charlie'.

Whilst no one really knows the origins of the legend, it is rumoured that the cause of these events is a former prisoner, who had been tortured before being executed for murder. These stories have been passed down by word of mouth over many years by the terrified staff that has worked there.

There is no record of anyone called Charles or Charlie being executed during the period the police occupied City Hall.

'Charlie' was a popular Bradford term of endearment or ridicule in Victorian times. The early night watchmen were sometimes referred to as 'Charlies', named after Charles II. Expressions such as 'he's a right Charlie!' was commonly used up until recent times. It is likely that the name 'Charlie' was given to the entity as a handle on which to pin the psychic events.

The 'Chains' part of the name seems to be related to the noise of chains, sometimes associated with the manifestation of poltergeist activity.

Psychic events came to a head in the 1980s, when they became so troublesome that council staff declined to work in certain areas on their own. In 1988 there were persistent accounts of paranormal activity.

Bradford Council's Information Officer reported a spate of ghostly activity, including objects and cupboards moving on their own, sudden cold spots and ghostly apparitions.

Another council official recounted sightings of mysterious shadows and of staff members being fearful of venturing alone into certain areas of City Hall. It was reported that on one occasion a cleaner had her mop taken from her by a ghostly entity. Sounds of court proceedings and rattling chains were also reported as coming from the old court rooms, even though they were not in use at the time.

From time to time since the year 2000, the West Yorkshire Police have reoccupied various areas of City Hall to establish contact points for members of the public in the city centre. This has coincided with what can only be described as poltergeist activity.

These peaks have often related to the comings and goings of the regular police and wardens and during structural alterations.

Incidents of paranormal activity in City Hall seem to have become particularly troublesome during major changes and in particular when the Police Museum was established.

THE POLICE MUSEUM

The Bradford Police Museum was founded in *2014* by former Police Inspector, Dr Martin Baines QPM who, along with his wife and his daughter, the curator Natalie Baines, created the exhibition centre and opened up the old charge office and cells. A number of former retired Bradford police officers returned to City Hall to become museum guides.

With the assistance of Bradford Council, the old A Division police area of the former City of Bradford Police, including the police cells, were restored. Victorian artefacts and exhibits from Victorian times are now on display. The old court room is also part of the museum experience. The museum was officially launched and opened up to public tours on 6th August, 2014.

During this period operational police officers, council wardens and community support officers also re-occupied the adjacent area. This period of change seemed to trigger an upsurge in psychic phenomena in City Hall.

In 2015, with other former retired colleagues, I became a volunteer guide, at the Bradford Police Museum. During my various stints as a guide I became aware of a number of reports of unexplained events occurring within City Hall, the police department and museum. Reports of alleged 'ghostly' occurrences, included flying objects, cold spots, and malfunctioning technology were recounted.

The ladies' toilets became the focus of unusual phenomena. A towel dispensing machine operating on its own: rattling out paper towels whilst an officer was in the cubicle. A ghostly figure was also seen in the mirror.

Members of the council security staff stationed in City Hall also reported phantom figures, as well as CCTV automatically tracking invisible entities. Phantom figures were reported going up the stairs. A Councillor was reportedly 'pushed' by an 'invisible force' whilst in the Mayor's Parlour and a large bull mastiff security dog refused to enter a certain passage at night. A Victorian phantom-like figure was also seen entering the Victorian toilets.

On an ongoing basis, visitors to the police cells experienced cold spots, seen shadows and felt a 'presence.'

'Snowstorms'
More recently orbs have been seen on City Hall video camera and a phantom figure captured on camera.

AN INVESTIGATION

My first reaction was that there would more than likely be more mundane explanations for these experiences.

However as more reports were received, the more intrigued I became. I eventually decided to investigate the reports.

The occurrences fell under the following categories of so called psychic phenomena also known as 'poltergeist' activity:

- Cold spots
- Electrical disturbances
- Mechanical objects working on their own
- Rapping or banging on walls or other unexplained noises
- Objects moving or being thrown around by themselves
- Objects mysteriously disappearing and reappearing
- Unusual smells

I took with me some basic equipment:

- Notebook and pen
- Camera
- Voice recorder
- Temperature gauge
- EMF gauge
- Years of investigative experience

NOTES: POLICE DEPARTMENT

My first visit was to the police department located at the eastern end of city hall. This block contains the police, council wardens and police community support officers.

Police officers had reported these events shortly after the museum had opened. Initially I felt somewhat constrained at even raising these matters as a serious topic of conversation. I was however pleasantly surprised at how open and freely they related their experiences to me.

Here are my notes...

Date: June 2014.

Witness: Police Officer.

Location: Police Department City Hall. Main police office.

Event/s: Empty water bottle 'flying' across room during briefing session.

Note: Convincing witness. Other reliable witnesses present.

> *None of us at the briefing could believe our eyes when the water bottle flew across the briefing room*

Date: May, 2014.

Witness: Police Officer.

Location: Police Department City Hall. Passageway and ladies toilet.

Event/s: Icy areas in passageway and toilets. Manual hand towel dispenser in toilets self-activating.

Note: Temperature normal range. Dispenser working OK. Experienced reliable witness.

Ladies toilet

Date: Various dates between May & December 2014

Witness: Police Officer.

Location: Police Department City Hall. Main police office.

Event/s: Computer screens malfunctioning, changing screen images, switching on and off. Desktop objects including pens going missing and re-appearing, window blinds moving without external influence.

Note: Convincing witness. Police computers checked, working normally.

Police department

Most of the accounts came from regular, experienced police officers; trained observers with their feet firmly on the ground. In assessing their reliability I took into account the following factors.

Police witnesses are generally considered to be honest, reliable, observers; and their evidence under normal circumstances would be accepted in a court of law.

Their accounts were consistent with the events witnessed by others from non-police backgrounds countering any claim of collusion.

They had no obvious motive for inventing these reports. On the contrary they risked ridicule and derision for making such claims.

They came across as genuine believable witnesses.

I concluded that the witnesses had clearly encountered events that were beyond their normal frame of reference. I am unable to explain these occurrences other than to describe them as so called 'poltergeist' activity.

Date: December, 2014.

Witness: Police Officer.

Location: Police Reception Point City Hall.

Event/s: 'Icy' patches. Hand bell flew off the desk. Also experienced same towel dispenser phenomena in toilet.

NOTES: CITY HALL AND COURTS

My investigation took me to the security office to interview the security guards employed at the City Hall. Their office is located at the west end of the building where they control access to City Hall. In their office they have a bank of CCTVs screens covering the entire interior of the building. They have responsibility for the security of City Hall.

I became aware of these reports from police officers who had been told of these accounts by security staff. My visits were at night, to enable me to witness any occurrences that might occur.

These are my brief notes...

Date: June, 2014.

Witness: Security Guard.

Location: City Hall.

Event/s: Automatic detector lighting activated in 'Lib Dem' areas. 'Running man' logo and CCTV cameras tracking 'invisible entities'.

Note: Verified auto lights and camera tracking activated. Nothing visible.

Date: December, 2014, 19:00.

Witness: Security Guard.

Location: City Hall.

Event/s: 'Phantom' lower body and legs climbing staircase.

Note: Witness admits being terrified. Appeared to have had a frightening experience.

Court area

Date: January, 2015, 22:00.

Witness: Security Guard.

Location: City Hall.

Event/s: Man in Victorian garb entering toilets inside City Hall. Outer doors secured.

Note: Convincing witness.

Date: December, 2014, 22:15.

Witness: Security Guard.

Location: City Hall.

Event/s: Guard dog terrified. Refused to enter passageway.

Note: Convincing witness.

Courts tunnel

Date: June 2015.

Witness: Security Guard.

Location: City Hall.

Event/s: Loud noises coming from the courts adjacent to the Chief Executive's Office. Investigation revealed court room empty. No longer a working court.

Note: Hearsay from third person. (Responding to request from CEO. Not interviewed)

> *The Chief Executive asked me what was all the noise coming from the courts . . . . . It was empty!*

Date: January 2015.

Witness: Security Guard.

Location: Room 136 City Hall.

Event/s: Councillor experienced a presence of some 'entity.' One person pushed to one side by an invisible force.'

Note: Hearsay from third person. Not verified.

Date: 23rd May 2015, 19:00.

Witness: Security Guard and Investigator.

Location: Cellars City Hall.

Event/s: Cold spots, shadows and 'orbs' experienced.

Note: The investigator and the security guard encountered drops in temperature. Image of 'orb' and shadows photographed.

City Hall cellars showing 'orb'

> *" The Chief Executive asked me what was all the noise coming from the courts . . . . . It was empty! "*

Dock and public gallery

Date: 12th September 2015, morning.

Witness: Museum Guide.

Location: Law Courts.

Event/s: PA system speakers malfunctioning during court room re-enactments. System subsequently abandoned during afternoon session.

Note: System not investigated for technical faults.

The witnesses were security guards with years of experience and considered honest and reliable.

NOTES: MUSEUM AND CELLS

The museum opened to the public in August *2014*, around the time a modern police contact point was established. It is on the eastern side of City Hall in the exact location of the original Victorian police station. The main museum exhibition is on the site of the old parade room. A passageway leads from the old police parade room to the charge desk and cells. The old law courts can be reached via a metal staircase from the cell area.

Visitors to the museum have the benefit of a personal guide, usually a former Bradford police officer.

The guides are down to earth retired police officers. They have enjoyed many years police experience and relate their personal experiences to the visitors. Since opening to the public a number of 'events' have occurred in the cell areas which I have also investigated.

These are my brief notes...

Date: 18th July 2015.

Witness: Guide.

Location: Cells.

Event/s: Voices, whispers coming from cell area. No one present.

Note: Experienced guide.

```
Date: 22nd August 2015.

Witness: Visitor.

Location: Cells.

Event/s: Sudden drop in temperature. Presence felt.

Note: Middle aged female. Credible witness.
```

> *It was icy cold and I felt I was being watched*

The cells

Date: 12th September 2015.

Witness: Guide.

Location: Cells.

Event/s: Shadowy figure passing in corridor. Visitor reported cold spot.

Note: Experienced, credible witness.

Date: 16th September 2015.

Witness: Guide.

Location: Cells.

Event/s: Smells of excrement and urine in two cells.

Note: Experienced guide. Cells were unsoiled and no unusual smells when re-checked.

The cells

Houdini's escape cell

Date: 12th September 2015.

Witness: 10 year old girl.

Location: Cells.

Event/s: Girl with alleged psychic powers experienced 'presence' of entity and cold in cell.

Note: Girl's claims vouched for by grandmother who was also present.

There have been a growing number of other comments by visitors on the tour regarding unsettling experiences. Not all of these have been recorded, as they have often put down to 'over active' imagination.

FINDINGS

Although a major building extension of City Hall was undertaken in 1909, all the unexplained activities that have persisted, have been confined to the original 1873 areas of what was the original Town Hall. These re-aligned areas seem particularly prone to these phenomena.

Most of these occurrences could generally be described as 'poltergeist' activity and have been reported in many different settings over many years. There is much debate over the nature of these occurrences. Are they caused by spirits and the ghosts of the dead, or are other more prosaic explanations for these phenomena?

Like the old court room the 'jury is still out.'

Whilst the true nature of these 'events' remains an open question, many credible witnesses, believe that 'Chains Charlie' continues to roam Bradford City Hall, perhaps longing for a return to the 'good' old days when Bradford had its own police force in City Hall.

*For the latest sightings visit **www.spectralbooks.com***

ABOUT THE AUTHOR

The author has enjoyed successful careers in the police service, health sectors, training, business and international affairs. He has also worked with local charities and is a much sought-after after dinner speaker.

He initially served in the former West Riding Constabulary in Shipley before transferring to Bradford City force in 1968. He worked both as a uniform Constable and a Detective from Bradford City Hall with personal experience of the old cells and court room.

Les became divisional commander for Bradford Central and helped establish various multi-agency initiatives including Drug Watch, Bradford Inner City Licensing Association and City Centre Beat. For a number of years he was also a senior visiting lecturer at the National Police Staff College at Bramshill.

Over the years he has taken a particular interest in Bradford's social history and in particular the City Hall.

He is currently a volunteer guide at the Bradford Police Museum, (Under the Clock) where, along with other colleagues, he shares police related anecdotes.

As a member of the Society of Psychical Research he has taken a keen interest in reports of paranormal activities.

His recent investigations into reports of paranormal activity are sometimes shared with the visitors to the Bradford Police Museum in City Hall.

APPENDIX 1: DEATHS IN CITY HALL

A TRAGIC HABIT

Joseph Hainsworth was a 40 year old Bradford surgeon who fell on hard times due to his growing dependency on alcohol and laudanum; a 19th century, opiate-based patent medicine.

The doctor first came to the notice of the police on the 21st September 1874, when he was arrested by PC Jenkins of the Bradford Borough Police for being drunk outside the Spotted Ox in Westgate. However on being searched at the charge desk an empty bottle labelled, 'Laudanum' was found in his possession and the police surgeon was called. Dr Parkinson found that Hainsworth was under the influence of laudanum and subsequently arranged to have his stomach pumped out. The drunkenness charge was not pursued. However he was later charged with attempted suicide, which was still a crime.

At the Borough Court, Hainsworth explained in his defence that he had legitimately acquired the 'medicine' from Rimmington's Chemist for medical reason and had accidentally overdosed. Mr Rimmington accepted that he had supplied the laudanum but thought nothing of it as he had previously supplied Dr Hainsworth with medicines when he had a successful practice. As a result he was acquitted of the charge.

On the Monday evening, of the 23rd May 1875, Joseph Hainsworth was discovered in the cellars at the Bradford Infirmary and the police were called. Coincidentally the same PC Jenkins attended. He arrested Dr Hainsworth for being found in the hospital cellar for unlawful purposes.

He was once again taken to the Town Hall where he was again placed in a police cell. The following day he was found in a collapsed condition. Despite the surgeon's best efforts he died at 2.45pm that afternoon from laudanum poisoning.

A DEATH IN POLICE CUSTODY

At nine o'clock, on a cold Monday evening on the 3rd October 1887, Police Constable Jones was on duty in the Bradford police charge office in the Town Hall, when James Hepworth, a 48 year old stone mason's clerk was brought into custody for breaking and entering a shop. He was searched and placed in a cell with a 13 year old boy.

At 12.25 am the following morning, PC Jones peered through the observation hatch of Hepworth's cell and was shocked to see the prisoner suspended in a kneeling position on the cell floor. His inert body was facing the cell wall with his arms hanging limply in front of him. His braces were fastened around his neck and attached to the cell bars. The boy was still asleep on the cell bench.

Superintendent Laycock was called out and the body cut down. His pockets were searched and a folded note to his sister was found saying: "I have gone to live and die up Legrams Lane. I thought I would end my troubles where they began - I mean Bob Ropers." Robert Roper was a local stone mason and the deceased's employer. It seems there had been some ill feeling between the two.

Hepworth's body was taken to the public mortuary where a Dr Lodge performed a post mortem examination and confirmed death was due to strangulation. The deceased's estranged wife, Sarah Hepworth, identified the body and reported that he had been drinking heavily and she had last seen him the previous Thursday when he appeared the worse for drink. When police visited Roper's office it was found to have been destroyed by fire. At the subsequent inquest, the jury returned a verdict that the deceased had committed suicide whilst 'temporarily insane.'

Although the facts of this case do not entirely fit the legend, it can be noted that the deceased did in fact die from hanging.

CHRISTMAS DAY TRAGEDY

By Christmas Day, 1918, the war to end all wars was over. The armistice had been signed some three weeks earlier and there was great rejoicing as surviving soldiers returned home to their loved ones.

One such soldier was Edmund Watson, a 21 year old former RAF gunner who had been twice wounded in battle. After his discharge he suffered from mental health problems as did many other discharged servicemen. This condition was often referred to as 'war worry.'

He became a suspect in an investigation into theft of jewellery and was subsequently arrested by Detective Chief Inspector Petty on Tuesday 24th December. At that time he had been receiving treatment at St Luke's Hospital, Bradford. After his arrival at the Town Hall he was lodged in one of the police cells pending the outcome of further enquires.

During the early hours of the following day PC Wood who was on duty in the charge office, visited the cells during his normal rounds and found Watson hanging from the pipes by two towels tied around his neck. He was pronounced dead by the police surgeon. The inquest found that he had 'committed suicide during temporary insanity.'

A TRAGIC AFFAIR

Vera Stonehouse, a 35 years old single woman, tragically met her death due to a failed abortion in May, 1939. The abortionist, Clara Louisa Hardy 62 years of age was committed for trial for manslaughter on the 21st November, 1939.

During the court proceedings Harry Gustav Borstel aged 33 years, a constable in the Bradford City Police and a married man, gave evidence at the hearing. He admitted being intimate with the deceased and being responsible for her subsequent pregnancy. He had since reconciled with his wife.

Police Constable Borstel, who had 15 years' service, worked in the police property store at City Hall. After leaving the court he returned to his duties at City Hall working with a colleague PC Spencer with whom he had worked for the past eight weeks.

About 3.10pm that afternoon, Borstel had gone into an adjoining office. A short time later there was the sound of a loud report from the room.

When PC Spencer investigated he found PC Borstal lying on the floor with a head wound and a service revolver near his left hand. He was removed to hospital where he subsequently died.

The inquest found that he had 'committed suicide during temporary insanity.'